a book in twenty-two chapters including one chapter that isn't
a chapter, mud, a pond, China, weasels, William Shakespeare's
name and an appendix (at no extra charge) by

MICHAEL ROSEN

UNCLE
GOBB

AND THE PLOT PLOT

with very excellent pictures full of
genies, weasels and baked beans by

NEAL LAYTON

BLOOMSBURY
CHILDREN'S BOOKS

LONDON   OXFORD   NEW YORK   NEW DELHI   SYDNEY

BLOOMSBURY CHILDREN'S BOOKS
Bloomsbury Publishing Plc
50 Bedford Square, London WC1B 3DP, UK

BLOOMSBURY, BLOOMSBURY CHILDREN'S BOOKS and the Diana logo
are trademarks of Bloomsbury Publishing Plc

First published in Great Britain in 2018 by Bloomsbury Publishing Plc

A catalogue record for this book is available from the British Library

ISBN: HB: 978-1-4088-7394-6; ebook: 978-1-4088-7396-0

2 4 6 8 10 9 7 5 3 1

Printed and bound in Great Britain by CPI Group (UK) Ltd, Croydon CR0 4YY

FSC
www.fsc.org
MIX
Paper from
responsible sources
FSC® C020471

To find out more about our authors and books visit www.bloomsbury.com
and sign up for our newsletters

For Emma, Elsie and Emile

CHAPTER 1

The Middle of the Night

It was the middle of the night.

If you have read what this chapter is called ('The Middle of the Night'), you already know that it was the middle of the night. If you didn't read what this chapter is called, you would have missed that it was called 'The Middle of the Night'. No worries, because now you do know that it was the middle of the night.

Malcolm was fast asleep.

He *was* fast asleep. Then, all of a sudden, he wasn't fast asleep. He was awake.

And it was still the middle of the night. No one likes waking up in the middle of the night. Apart from owls.

A NOTE ON OWLS:

They wake up, fly about, catch mice, eat them, and then a few hours later, do a sicky thing where bits of the mice they've eaten come back up again.

I'm not telling you this for any old reason.

I'm telling you this because this is what Malcolm was lying awake thinking about. He was asking himself, *WHY do owls sick up bits of mice?*

He lay on his back, staring at the ceiling. And he remembered the words 'owl pellets' from a book he read called '**Great Owl Pellets of the World**'. *Imagine,* he thought, *if instead of that time when I was on TV and the man asked me what was the capital of Italy and I said,* **'Ponky'** *... what if, instead of that, the man had asked me, 'What is the proper name for owl sick?' I could have said, 'Owl pellets!' and I would have been right.*

Ah, if only.

Just then the dog barked.

Wow, thought Malcolm, still lying on his back in bed, *that IS strange. I told him not to bark. I remember quite clearly saying to him, 'Don't bark tonight.' And there he is barking.*

Then Malcolm heard a dragging sound. Something was being dragged.

The dog barked again, and following that, someone or something said, 'Shh!'

Then came the dragging sound again.

All that interesting stuff about owl pellets just flew out of Malcolm's mind.

(You probably don't want to think about owl pellets flying out of someone's mind, so if you don't want to, just stop thinking about it. If Malcolm had been thinking about weasels, they would have flown out of his mind too.)

 Weasel 1: Hello again.

 Weasel 2: Looks like we're back again, with our weasel words.

 Weasel 1: No, we don't say weasel words, remember?

 Weasel 2: Don't we?

 Weasel 1: No, we're weasels. It's humans

who say weasel words, not weasels. We don't actually talk. Except when people like Neal Layton do drawings of us talking.

Weasel 2: Oh yes, I remember: we don't talk. By the way, what are weasel words?

Weasel 1: That was explained in another *Uncle Gobb* book. If you really want to know, just look it up in there.

Weasel 2: All right, all right. No need to get ratty about it.

Weasel 1: I'm not being ratty. I'm not a rat. I'm a weasel.

Weasel 2: Me too. I'm a weasel.

Weasel 1: I know you're a weasel. You don't need to tell me you're a weasel.

Then came the dragging sound again.

Malcolm waited for the dog to bark.

The dog didn't bark that time.

Aha, thought Malcolm, *me telling the dog not to bark has worked. The dog did after all listen carefully, has remembered what I said and is now doing what I told him to do. Which is not bark.*

Then came the dragging sound again.

Malcolm decided that the dragging sound was scary.

Malcolm remembered a horror story he read once about a giant cucumber. It wasn't a living cucumber. It was a dead cucumber that had become a ghost. And in the middle of the night, this ghost-cucumber couldn't sleep.

So it walked about the house dragging something. *I think it was chains,* Malcolm thought *... but then why would a ghost-cucumber be dragging chains? If there was a ghost-cucumber dragging something, surely it would be something that cucumbers hang out with, like a bit of lettuce?*

The sound that Malcolm could hear downstairs was not the sound of a ghost-cucumber dragging a bit of lettuce. It sounded more like a chair being dragged – yes – his chair, the little, funny wood-and-metal chair he had had ever since he was little and funny.

When Malcolm was three, he remembered, he went to a place every day called 'Start', but then it closed, and when it closed, they

said people could take a chair home instead.
Malcolm found his chair, took it home and he
had kept it ever since. The dog liked sleeping on
it. Or under it.

HERE IS AN IMPORTANT MESSAGE

If you wake up in the middle of the night and you start to hear things, sometimes you say things to yourself that are not totally sensible. That's because you might be half asleep.

END OF IMPORTANT MESSAGE

The next thing that Malcolm thought was most definitely *not* a sensible thing to think. What he said to himself was, *Oh, my chair is going out for a walk.*

Then there was a crash, and a voice said, 'OH BLUE BLUE BLUE!'

Malcolm knew immediately who said, 'OH BLUE BLUE BLUE!' It was Uncle Gobb. Uncle Gobb was the only person he knew

who said **'OH BLUE!'** when something bad
happened.

But why was Uncle Gobb dragging his chair around in the middle of the night?

Malcolm got up, went downstairs, switched on the light and looked at Uncle Gobb.

Uncle Gobb was definitely dragging the chair.

Aha! said Malcolm to himself.

Uncle Gobb's up to something again. He's already tried to get rid of me and my bestest friend Crackersnacker by shoving us in the **DREAD SHED***. He's already tried to get rid of me and my bestest friend Crackersnacker in America ... but we DEFEATED HIM!!!! I know I can defeat him again, so this time I'll find out what his plan is straight away. No hanging about.*

Malcolm took a step forward, towards Uncle Gobb, and said, 'Uncle Gobb, why are you moving my chair in the middle of the night?'

Uncle Gobb – who at the very exact moment that Malcolm switched on the light was moving Malcolm's chair in the middle of the night – said, 'I'm not moving your chair in the middle of the night.'

Malcolm's teacher, Mr Keenly, once said something really interesting about things like this. He said that when someone says something that everyone knows is not true, it's because there's something else altogether that they don't want you to know. So, Malcolm thought this through: If Mr Keenly is right, then Uncle Gobb isn't really trying to tell me that he's not moving my chair in the middle of the night; he knows he's moving my chair in the middle of the night; he knows *I know* he's moving my chair in the middle of the night; there's something else altogether that he doesn't want me to know about. This is what my greatest, bestest most brilliantest friend, Crackersnacker, would call 'The Something Else Thing'.

CHAPTER 2

The Something Else Thing

While we're waiting for Malcolm to find out what **The Something Else Thing** could be, we could spend a few moments together trying to figure it out for ourselves.

Here's a list of possibles:

1. Uncle Gobb is going to move Malcolm's chair next to the cupboard, stand on it, and get some baked beans out of the cupboard.

2. Uncle Gobb has a secret collection of chairs that he doesn't want anyone to know

about. In the middle of the night, he woke up and started to think about Malcolm's chair downstairs. He got up and started to drag it away to put in Gobb's Secret Chair Museum.

3. Uncle Gobb is going to take it to China. Quite often Uncle Gobb says, 'I'VE BEEN TO CHINA.' Now he's going to go back to China and he's going to take the chair.

4. Uncle Gobb thinks that Malcolm — and his great friend Crackersnacker — are not doing enough homework and not learning anywhere near enough for the tests. This makes him really, really, really angry. Uncle Gobb is moving the chair to put in front of the door, so that when Malcolm gets up in the morning, he won't be able to get out, and Uncle Gobb can start the day with some really good questions, like: 'What is William Shakespeare's name?'

5. It's not a very long list, is it? And yet it is the end of the list.

CHAPTER 3

The Something Else Thing (Again.)

Malcolm looked very hard at Uncle Gobb as he was moving his chair. The dog looked very hard at Uncle Gobb as he was moving Malcolm's chair.

Malcolm, who you'll remember is not going to put up with any more of Uncle Gobb's secret plans to get rid of him and Crackersnacker, again said, 'Uncle Gobb, why are you moving my chair?'

Uncle Gobb raised his hand in the air, breathed in and said, 'Ah, yes, that's one of your questions, isn't it, Malcolm? Yes, it is. It's a question. It's the kind of question that's very like a question. In fact, it's not only like a question, it *is* a question. Well done, Malcolm.'

'Uncle Gobb,' Malcolm said sternly, 'why are you moving my chair?'

Just then, Mum walked in. Her eyes were almost shut.

Uncle Gobb looked as if Mum walking in was something he really didn't want to happen.

'Derek,' said Mum, 'why are you moving Malcolm's chair in the middle of the night?'

Uncle Gobb looked to and fro, started to go red, suddenly found that he had got a wedgie, tried to get the wedgie out, scratched his head, cleared his throat, cleared his throat again and said, 'I need it, Tessa.'

Malcolm thought of Uncle Gobb trying to sit down, and squeezing into his little chair.

'But your bum will get stuck,' Malcolm said.

Mum took a different line. Malcolm knew that Mum tried to look after Uncle Gobb. She was Uncle Gobb's sister after all. Malcolm knew that no matter how horrible Uncle Gobb was, he needed Mum to look after him and Mum was kind enough to do so.

'Well, Derek,' she said as kindly as she could, 'Malcolm likes that chair. The dog likes that chair. You can't just take it.'

Uncle Gobb went on standing in the middle of the room clearing his throat and removing wedgies, or imaginary wedgies.

INTERESTING NOTE

In the book 'Imagine the Imaginary', under the letter 'I', it has 'Imaginary Wedgies: an imaginary wedgie is the wedgie you think you have when you are feeling awkward. No matter how hard you try to get rid of the imaginary wedgie, it goes on being an imaginary wedgie. Famous people who have had imaginary wedgies include Jeremiah Worksheet, who invented the worksheet 'Henry VIII; Reggie Wedgie'.

29

'Well, Derek,' Mum said, 'the best thing for all of us, I think, is if you head off back to bed, hmmm?'

Just then, a voice outside said, in an 'I'm-trying-to-be-quiet' voice, 'Ready when you are, Derek.'

Mum looked at Uncle Gobb, then went over to the back door, opened it, and looked out.

A man with a very thick neck and wearing gloves was standing there. Straight away, he stepped forward and made a move to take Malcolm's little chair. Uncle Gobb shook his head very hard, as if to say, 'Don't do it!'

The man stopped in his tracks. He could see that something wasn't right. Mum – whose eyes were now a little bit more open – looked from one to the other. Malcolm looked past the man to something outside.

Outside was the **DREAD SHED!!!!!** IF YOU KNOW WHAT THE **DREAD SHED** IS, YOU CAN MISS OUT THE NEXT CHAPTER. IF YOU DON'T KNOW WHAT THE **DREAD SHED** IS, YOU TOO CAN MISS

OUT THE NEXT CHAPTER, BUT THEN YOU WON'T KNOW WHAT THE **DREAD SHED** IS. YOU MIGHT THINK IT'S A KIND OF GHOST-CUCUMBER. OR A SHED WITH DREADLOCKS. OR A SHED THAT WAS SUPPOSED TO BE THE RED SHED BUT SOMEONE CALLED IT THE **DREAD SHED** BY MISTAKE. IT'S UP TO YOU.

CHAPTER 4

The DREAD SHED

There is only one **DREAD SHED** in the world and it belongs to Uncle Gobb. Once, he put Malcolm and his great friend Crackersnacker in the **DREAD SHED**, but they found the way out of the **DREAD SHED** by walking through the door.

Oh, yes we did! thought Malcolm.

You wouldn't want to go in the **DREAD SHED**. It's very dark inside. It has cobwebs and smells of wee.

Once, long ago, there used to be many **DREAD SHEDS** – all created in order to lock away poor, bad children – but people thought the **DREAD SHEDS** weren't nice, so they got rid of them. Except for little Derek Gobb, who saved one **DREAD SHED**. And the **DREAD SHED** standing outside the back door at this very moment was the one that little Derek Gobb had saved, long

LITTLE DEREK GOBB

before he became Uncle Gobb, long before his
marriage with Tammy went **BLAMMM!!**
and they broke up, and long before he came to
stay with Mum and Malcolm.

Dog: And me. He came to stay with me too.

Weasel 2: And us.

Weasel 1: We don't actually live with
Malcolm, Mum, Uncle Gobb and the dog. We
live in this book.

Weasel 2: Isn't that the same thing as
living with Malcolm, Mum, Uncle Gobb and the
dog?

Weasel 1: No.

The **DREAD SHED** has little wheels on the bottom, so it can be moved about. The wheels don't make it nice. They're just wheely sort of wheels that do wheely things.

Malcolm and Crackersnacker made up a song about the wheels. They said that it wasn't meant to be a cool song sung by people who wear sunglasses indoors. They said that they made it up for very small children to clap along to.

'We're the little wheels doing really wheely things,
We wheel along wheelily singing wheely sings,
We're really wheely wheels going round and
round and round
but people in shops calls us "castors".
Booooooooo!'

CHAPTER 5

In a Car Park?
(But still in the room in the middle of the night with Uncle Gobb and his imaginary wedgies and the man with the thick neck wearing gloves. (It's not his neck that's wearing gloves. It's the man with the thick neck. He's wearing gloves on his hands.))

Mum stopped being nice.

She didn't stop being a nice person. She stopped being nice to Uncle Gobb. She could see that something very, very dodgy was going on. Malcolm could see it too.

'Who are you?' Mum asked the man with gloves on.

'Roald Dahl,' said the man.

Malcolm stared.

'You wrote *Charlie and the Chocolate Factory*,' Malcolm blurted out.

'No, not me,' said the man. 'That was the other Roald Dahl. I'm Roald Dahl Removals.'

'No, you're not,' said Mum. 'I've seen you before. You're one of Derek's little friends from 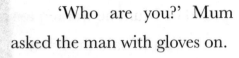 that he belongs to.'

(At moments like this, Malcolm felt so

proud of Mum he wanted to squeeze her.)

'Am I?' said the man.

'Who are you?' Mum asked.

'Fred Shed,' he said.

'Well, Fred,' said Mum, 'for starters, I don't believe you're Fred Shed, but it's too late for me to care either way. Could you just step away from Malcolm's chair? And you, Derek, step away too. The chair is not going anywhere.'

Malcolm said, 'The chair is not going anywhere.'

He knew that Mum had already said, 'The chair is not going anywhere,' but it sounded like such a great thing to say, he just felt he had to say it himself.

Mum went on. 'I can see that you've moved your little dready sheddy thing up to the door. You, Fred, on your way out, can move it back to where it was before. Meanwhile, we can all go to bed.'

'So we're not putting the chair in the school, then?' Fred Shed said.

Uncle Gobb's eyes were making huge *Don't Say Anything* signs at Fred Shed.

...Don't say Anything Sign... Don't Say Anything Sign... Don't Say Anything Sign...

The dog looked at the *Don't Say Anything* sign and thought about biting Fred Shed's leg.

Mum put her hands on her hips.

Malcolm looked at his lovely little chair that reminded him of happy times at his 'Start' nursery when they ate orange segments and sang 'Wind the Bobbin Up'.

'Were you going to take my chair to a school somewhere?' Malcolm asked.

41

'No, no,' said Fred Shed smilingly, and pointed at the **DREAD SHED**. 'This *is* the school.'

Malcolm looked at everyone round the room. He suddenly saw what was going on here. This was Uncle Gobb's big, new plan. He couldn't wait to tell Crackersnacker about it in the morning. Unbelievable. And Crackersnacker would say … What would he say? … He would say, 'The **DREAD SHED** is going to be an Uncle Gobb school???? *The* Uncle Gobb School!!! This is huge, Ponkyboy! This is massive!'

'The **DREAD SHED** is a school????
The Uncle Gobb School???!!!' Malcolm asked
everyone in the room. 'This is huge! This is
massive!'

But, Malcolm thought to himself,
*not so massive that Crackersnacker and I can't
handle it.*

Uncle Gobb tried to stop the conversation
getting any worse for him. He was going
red and getting sweaty. He lifted both hands
in the air and his voice was getting
squeaky.

'Tess, look … erm … you see … It's not
exactly like that –'

'Actually, it *is* like that,' said Fred Shed,

trying to be helpful. 'You see, Derek came to us at THE COW CLUB with the idea of setting up a school, and hey, here we are and we're up and running. BOM, BOM, TISH!'

NOTE ON BOM, BOM, TISH!

'Bom, bom, tish!' comes from a book called 'Great Things to Say When You Want to Sound as If The Thing You're Going to Do Next Is Really Easy'.

'A school?' said Mum. 'A school? Oh I see what's going on here ... it was all going fine but then you discovered that you didn't have any chairs for your little school????' she continued, piecing it all together and starting to laugh.

44

'So you thought you would take Malcolm's chair … and … and …' She ran out of steam, thinking of how crazy the whole thing was, but Malcolm was piecing it all together too.

'You can't have a school in the **DREAD SHED**, Uncle Gobb,' he said. 'It smells of wee.'

'Look, Tess, I was going to tell you …' said Uncle Gobb.

'Hang on,' said Malcolm, feeling good about sorting this out, 'if it was my chair you were taking, then you should have asked *me*.'

Uncle Gobb carried on talking (and going red). '… but the point is, I know lots of important things. I'VE BEEN TO CHINA. It's not easy finding a place to make a school. By no means. Then I remembered my DREAD SHED.

Well remembered, Derek, I said to myself. Perfect. I've been talking to  people. Friends. People people.

My ge–'

Then he stopped. Right in the middle of talking. As if he had got something stuck in his throat. Like a baked bean.

Malcolm noticed that Uncle Gobb had stopped himself saying something there ... something that began with 'gee'.

Then Uncle Gobb cleared the baked bean (or whatever it was) and, with a fiery gleam in his eyes, started up again. 'And it's going really well. I know that not everything I do goes well. Once, back in the good days, I created

GOBB EDUCATION™ .

But then, an evil man took it away from me. But I, Derek Gobb, can never be knocked down. That's why I'm starting a school. It's going to be a school where we do all the **important facts**. Any fact that isn't important is going to be thrown out. Or given a

detention. It's true we haven't got any chairs …
but we're putting my school in a school car park.
That way my **DREAD SHED** pupils can use
the toilets of the school.'

'What school?' said Malcolm.

'Your school,' said Uncle Gobb.

'My school!' said Malcolm. It was all getting
seriously more crazy. Malcolm loved his school.
He loved his teacher Mr Keenly, and he loved his
assistant teacher Janet, and he loved it that Janet
loved Mr Keenly. What was
this about some Uncle Gobb
school using his school? It all
sounded nasty. Even nastier
than a ghost-cucumber.

'Look here, you lot,' said Fred Shed, interrupting them and stepping further inside. 'I want to get this thing done and dusted. Can we stop faffing about? Let's bung the silly chair in the **DREAD SHED** and get the whole shebang up to the car park. C'mon, chop chop!'

'It's not a silly chair,' Malcolm said defiantly.

He looked at Mum. Surely she wasn't going to let this happen?

She wasn't going to let this happen.

'Stop right there, Fred Shed,' she said. 'The chair is staying right where it is. You are going to leave this house, right now. And don't come back. Ever. You, Derek, are going to go

back to your nice, warm bed with your favourite
teddy. Shoo!'

Fred Shed walked out.

'And move the **DREAD SHED** back
to where it was, on your way out,' she called
after him.

Mum closed the door. Uncle Gobb went back to bed, where his favourite teddy was

waiting for him. Mum put her arm round Malcolm and walked him back to his bed too, as the sound of the **DREAD SHED** being moved back into place came through the windows.

Hmmm, Malcolm thought, as he snuggled down in bed, *that Fred Shed man ... he looked like ... he looked like ... He looked a bit like someone I've seen before ... but which someone ... and which bit ... ?*

The dog barked, then remembered what Malcolm had said about not barking, thought about saying sorry, but fell asleep instead. On the chair.

 Weasel 2: Are we **important facts**?

Weasel 1: No.

Weasel 2: Does that mean we'll be thrown out or put in detention?

Weasel 1: We're not in the **DREAD SHED**. We're not at Uncle Gobb's **DREAD SHED SCHOOL**. We can't be thrown out of a place we're not in. You have to be *in* a place first if you're going to get thrown *out* of that place.

Weasel 2: Oh yes, I didn't think of that.

As Malcolm dozed off, he thought, *Well, Mum's sorted it all out. That's good.*

But then bit by bit, a strange, unsettled, scary feeling came over him. In his mind's eye, he could see Uncle Gobb right there, all day, every day, with his **DREAD SHED SCHOOL** in the school car park … as well as him already being there every morning, and every evening, and weekends.

Uncle Gobb and his weird helper, Fred Shed, would probably try to take other stuff for the **DREAD SHED SCHOOL**. *Not just the chair. Maybe the table. The baked beans. Maybe the whole house! Uncle Gobb was just … too close … too much right there … too much everywhere … too much in MY HEAD!*

Malcolm thought he would have to talk to
Crackersnacker about how to stop all this stuff
happening. If Dad was here, he wouldn't let it
happen, but Dad – huh! – Dad was up a tree
somewhere in America.

CHAPTER 6

A Floor

'Hi, guys!' said Dad.

It was six thirty in the morning and Dad was on the doorstep with a girl who was a bit younger than Malcolm. Malcolm knew she was called Lizard because he had met her when he met up with Dad in America.

Malcolm thought she was called Lizard because she collected lizards and could wiggle in the mud like a lizard. She also liked reading books called 'Great Lizards of the World'.

'Aren't you in America?' said Malcolm.

'No, buddy,' said Dad, scooping up Malcolm and giving him a big bear-hug, 'I'm here. Are you going to let us in?'

'Hi, Malc,' said Lizard and stepped forward to kiss him on the cheek.

Malcolm waited until that was over and said, 'Uncle Gobb tried to steal my chair.'

'Is Tess up yet?' Dad said, as he put Malcolm down and walked in.

Before Malcolm could answer or think,

Dad was rushing about, opening and closing cupboards, opening and closing the fridge, making himself coffee, pouring out cornflakes, making toast and heating up baked beans.

The whole point, Malcolm thought, *of going to America was to get rid of Uncle Gobb and*

bring back Dad ... That was 'The Swap'. But then the swap didn't happen. It had all been very, very disappointing. So what's all this? What's going on? Why is Dad here now? And are Dad and Lizard going to eat five tins of baked beans? Really?????!!!!

Weasel 1: That's a lot of beans.

Weasel 2: I love baked beans.

Weasel 1: No, you don't. You like eating flies.

Weasel 2: Oh yes.

Just then, Mum walked in.

'So what's all this?' she said.

'We're not staying, Tess,' Dad said. 'Don't worry. It's just that I thought we should stop by, say hi, and, hey, did you get my message?'

'What message?' said Mum.

'The message you didn't get,' said Dad. 'Look, it's like this …'

And he went off on a long tale about the summer camps for kids he was setting up –

Malcolm had seen one of them in America in the summer – and how he'd just been asked to set up one or two in England as well, so he'd be over for a while, which was great, wasn't it, because he would get to see Malcolm, and hang out, and chill and … and … and … eh, Tess, hmmm?

Malcolm watched while Dad ate the last of the cornflakes and Lizard ate the last of the Crumbles bars, and he wondered why things

never happened in quite the way he thought they should happen. It was great to see Dad, but then how long was he going to stay, and would Dad be around, nearby, while he was here in England? Or wandering all over England, looking for places to start up his camps?

Then Uncle Gobb walked in.

'Fender!' said Uncle Gobb in a surprised, annoyed, snobby way.

'Derek!' said Dad in a not-surprised, not-annoyed, not-snobby way, and Dad went up to Uncle Gobb and gave him a big hug, which Uncle Gobb hated more than he hated people who didn't know that William Shakespeare was William Shakespeare's name.

'When are you going?' said Uncle Gobb, having just noticed that Fender and Lizard had finished off his favourite strawberry jam.

When are YOU going? Malcolm thought, as he looked at Uncle Gobb.

'Come on, man,' said Dad, 'we're birds of passage, we're flying through. I thought that one of you could help us find a floor to sleep on for a few days while we get ourselves somewhere to stay.'

The moment Dad said 'floor', a picture came into Malcolm's mind. It was the picture of a floor. Not any old floor. Not a floor in the book 'Great Floors of the World'. It was the floor of the **DREAD SHED**.

'Yes,' said Mum. 'Give me a few minutes and I might be able to think of something, but I haven't woken up yet. We were disturbed in the night,' she added, looking very hard at Uncle Gobb.

The dog looked very hard at Uncle Gobb too.

'He's not staying here,' said Uncle Gobb. 'Nor is the girl.'

Lizard didn't seem bothered very much with anything that was going on around her. She was tickling the dog, who thought that being tickled was great.

Malcolm said, 'If you're looking for a floor, there's the floor of the **DREAD SHED**.'

In the 'Dictionary of the Very Worst Things to Say', what Malcolm said just then would have been near the beginning of the dictionary as one of the very, very, very, very worst things to say. The moment Malcolm said it, there was an explosion.

If you have read any other books about Uncle Gobb, you can guess what exploded. Yes, it was Uncle Gobb.

'How dare you?' he shouted at Malcolm. 'How dare you, boy?

That **DREAD SHED** is mine and mine alone. What's more, it is about to become more, oh so much more, than the **DREAD SHED**. As you very well know, it's about to become The **DREAD SHED SCHOOL**. Our first pupils are spick and span and ready to start on what will become a great adventure: an adventure with really **important facts** and really **rich knowledge**. The **DREAD SHED SCHOOL** will be rich with knowledge.'

'But they haven't got anything to sit on,' Malcolm said in a giggly, Crackersnackery sort of a way, 'which is why you were trying to steal my chair, remember?'

Uncle Gobb's arms started to wave about in several different directions at the same time.

He was furious Malcolm had said the thing about the chair in front of everyone; he was furious Dad had turned up; he was furious Lizard had turned up; he was furious Malcolm had suggested they could sleep in the **DREAD SHED**.

That was a lot of furiousness to be furious with. Here is a picture of a lot of furiousness:

In the end, after all that furiousness, the only thing that came out of Uncle Gobb's mouth was, 'IT'S MY **DREAD SHED**. IT'S MY **DREAD SHED**!'

But you haven't got a genie, Malcolm thought to himself as he remembered that Uncle Gobb's genie, Doctor Roop the Doop, had got fed up with Uncle Gobb not listening to him and had left. Without his genie, Uncle Gobb was useless and hopeless and would be easier than ever to defeat.

Mum said, 'Well, it may be yours, Derek, but at the moment, it's parked in my back yard and you haven't got anywhere else to put it. So, if I decide that it's OK for Fender and Lizard to kip in there for a night or two, there's not much you can do about it.'

Uncle Gobb stood up and shouted very, very loudly, 'I'VE BEEN TO CHINA. In China they know about calculus. Do you know about calculus, Malcolm?'

Malcolm hated Uncle Gobb firing questions at him, but this time he thought Uncle Gobb had got something wrong. *Surely he means 'octopus'. Or 'calculator' ... But then what if octopuses in China play with calculators and that's called 'calculus'?*

So Malcolm said, 'Do octopuses in China play with calculators?'

Uncle Gobb smacked his head and started shouting, 'No, no, no, no, no, no, no, no, no, no, no!!!!!! This is why we're falling behind,

Tessa ... but soon, thanks to me, we're going to CATCH UP!'

'That's lovely, Derek,' said Mum, pretending she hadn't heard Uncle Gobb ever say this sort of thing before. 'Now, if you could pop round to the shop and get us a loaf of bread, that would be lovely too.'

While Uncle Gobb went off to buy a loaf of bread, Dad and Lizard said it was very kind of Tess to let them move into the **DREAD SHED**, and that they had bed rolls and sleeping bags. Malcolm told them they might need to clean it up a bit because someone must have done a wee in there.

Not me.

Malcolm was wondering if Uncle Gobb might go into the shop and a little hand would come out of the loaf of bread, grab Uncle Gobb and drag him into the bread, and he would never be seen again. Ever.

He also wondered if one playtime would be time enough to tell Crackersnacker about everything that had happened since yesterday. Or if it would need two playtimes or three or four or five. He would just have to get to school and find out.

CHAPTER 7

English

'Right, class,' said Mr Keenly, 'we have a new girl joining us today. She's come from America and her name is Lizard.'

Ulla and Spaghetti said that they wanted Lizard to come and sit on their table and they could help her learn English.

'Thanks! Cool!' said Lizard. 'And I can tell you about lizards.'

As Lizard sat down with them, Ulla and Spaghetti whispered about how she seemed to speak English really well.

Malcolm looked at Lizard across the room and he had a sudden, amazing thought. It was the biggest amazing thought he had had since – well, since he discovered that by rubbing his nose a genie called the Genie of Malcolm's Nose could appear.

CHAPTER 8

The Very Big Amazing Thought

Perhaps you've had this amazing thought before Malcolm had it. This sometimes happens when we read books or watch movies. I mean, when I read 'Three Little Pigs' for the first time, I had the amazing thought that the wolf was going to turn into a pig.

← MY AMAZING THOUGHT

Then I remembered it was called the THREE little pigs, not the FOUR little pigs, so I let that idea drop.

Malcolm's amazing thought was about Lizard.

Is Lizard my sister? he wondered.

MALCOLM'S AMAZING THOUGHT

CHAPTER 9

It Doesn't Belong to Anyone!

When Malcolm had amazing thoughts, he liked to share them with Crackersnacker. So, while Ulla and Spaghetti were discussing whether Lizard spoke English or not, Malcolm turned to Crackersnacker and said, 'I think she's my sister.'

Crackersnacker looked at Lizard and looked back at Malcolm. 'That's amazing, Ponkyboy,' he said. 'That's really, really amazing. Does anyone else know?'

'I don't know,' said Malcolm. 'That's something we're going to have to find out.'

'Yes,' said Crackersnacker.

'And I've got loads and loads and loads more to tell you. Really amazing stuff.'

'Great,' said Crackersnacker, nodding some big nods.

Just then, Mr Keenly clapped his hands together three times. And Janet, the assistant teacher, helpfully led everyone into clapping their hands together three times back at Mr Keenly. Everyone did it, apart from Lizard. Ulla and Spaghetti explained to Lizard that this was how Mr Keenly got everyone to sit still and listen, so she clapped her hands three times

too. All on her own. No one minded though. Not even Mr Keenly, who looked at Lizard and smiled at her in a kind way. And Janet smiled at Mr Keenly even though Mr Keenly wasn't actually smiling at her.

'Now, class,' said Mr Keenly, 'I want to tell you about something very exciting. Hands up who knows the pond behind the fence at the end of the school field?'

Most people put their hands up.

Crackersnacker started giggling. Then he whispered to Malcolm, 'It's like he's saying the pond is a person. Do you know the pond? Sure I know the pond and the pond knows me. We're old friends. Hi, Pond!' Then Crackersnacker put on a pond voice and said, 'Hi, Crackersnacker!'

'It seems,' said Mr Keenly very keenly, 'that the pond doesn't BELONG to anyone!'

When he said 'BELONG', Mr Keenly opened his eyes wide, did a wiggly underliney thing in the air with his finger and pushed his mouth forward.

'But,' he went on, 'Janet and I and Mrs Office have been asking questions and sending letters, and if we are very, very lucky, that pond and the land around it — we call it a "**PLOT OF LAND**" — could end up being something that belongs to the school and that we could all use. I want you to spend the next twenty-nine seconds thinking of anything at all that we could use the pond and the **PLOT OF LAND** for …'

Everyone started thinking.

Lizard thought she could find lizards there.

Ulla thought they could stand in the pond.

Spaghetti thought they could find a dragon in the pond.

Freddy thought they could make mud.

Singalong thought they could make paper darts, climb the trees and throw the darts to see how far they would go,

EEEEEEEEEEOOOOOOOOWWWWWWWW.

Crackersnacker thought they could cover the pond in AstroTurf.

Malcolm thought they could dig a tunnel under it and put Uncle Gobb in the tunnel.

'Twenty-nine seconds up!' said Mr Keenly, and he listened to what people had thought.

'Lizards,' said Lizard.

Everyone turned round and looked at Lizard.

'Well, yes,' said Mr Keenly. 'Er … we might not call them that here, Lizard, but yes, there may be lizards.'

'Yup,' said Lizard, 'an' frogs an' toads an' bugs.'

'And dragons,' said Spaghetti.

'Well, yes and no,' said Mr Keenly, 'but let's not run ahead of ourselves. For the moment, we don't know for absolute certain it's going to be ours. There's still one or two things that have to be APPROVED.' (Wiggly underliney

thing in the air, big eyes, mouth pushed forward.)

Malcolm put up his hand.

'Yes, Malcolm?'

'My uncle says there's going to be a school in the car park.'

Some of the children started to giggle. Malcolm was quite well known in the class for saying things that sounded a bit strange.

A shadow crossed Mr Keenly's face. It seemed he didn't want to hear about the car park or Uncle Gobb's school. He put his lips together and looked like he didn't know what to say. Then the shadow passed, and Mr Keenly clapped his hands, and said, 'Literacy!'

Today, they had to write five sentences, each one beginning with words like 'first' or 'next' or 'later' or 'before' or 'much later' or 'afterwards' or 'eventually'.

Malcolm wondered if something could be 'much next'. Or 'eventually first'. Or 'afterwards later'. Or 'before before'. Looking out of the window, he could just see the pond and the little **PLOT OF LAND** ... and wasn't there the kind of grass in there that you could use to make arrows? Eventually. Or afterwards. Or first next ... ??? The tunnel to put Uncle Gobb in could have a glass panel over the top so you could look down and see what he was doing ... Next. Later. Before afterwards.

*

At playtime, Malcolm and Crackersnacker were just about to get in a little huddle, ready for Malcolm to tell him about everything that had happened, when Lizard came to join them.

'Hi,' she said.

'Hi,' they said.

Malcolm didn't know what to say.

He felt awkward. Not awkward enough to try and get rid of an imaginary wedgie, but still awkward.

But Crackersnacker said, 'Malc's just about to say what's been happening.'

'Great,' said Lizard.

As no one moved, or said anything else, and no imaginary wedgies turned up, Crackersnacker said, 'Go on then, Malc.'

So Malcolm talked and talked and talked about everything that had happened. As he listened, Crackersnacker slapped his side, laughed, frowned, nodded and shook his head and said, 'Wow, Ponkyboy!'

There was so much new stuff to take in in one go.

And the **DREAD SHED SCHOOL** in the car park sounded bad, Crackersnacker thought.

REALLY BAD.

'That's really bad, Ponkyboy,' he said. 'It would be like an invasion of **facts**. What I mean is, these kids and teachers and Uncle Gobb would come out of the **DREAD SHED SCHOOL** in the car park, piling into our toilets every day, going, **"HERE IS A FACT, HERE IS A FACT, HERE IS A FACT."**' When Crackersnacker said, '**HERE IS A FACT,**' he put on a robot voice. Still in a robot voice, he said, **'GIVE ME YOUR CHAIR, GIVE ME YOUR CHAIR. I MUST HAVE YOUR CHAIR. AND YOUR TABLE.'**

Lizard asked questions.

'This Fred Shed guy,' she said. 'Where do you think you've seen him before?'

No, Malcolm couldn't remember. It just made him a bit uncomfortable thinking about it.

And Uncle Gobb trying to steal his chair. That made him uncomfortable too. Or worse. Just a tiny bit scared.

Maybe Uncle Gobb would try again. What did they think? Yes, he could. Crackersnacker thought so. Lizard thought so too.

Was it worth planning how to get rid of Uncle Gobb again?

(Malcolm explained to Lizard how he had tried to get rid of Uncle Gobb twice before. Once was when he had met Lizard in America and he had hoped that there would be a swap between Dad and Uncle Gobb.)

'Yeah, but Fender has to look after me,' said Lizard.

'Does he?' said Malcolm.

'Yeah,' said Lizard.

That was nearly an Imaginary Wedgie Moment. As neither Crackersnacker nor Malcolm dared ask Lizard if

Fender was her dad or not, there wasn't much more to say about that for the time being. But they did look at each other with a special Malcolm-Crackersnacker 'this-could-be-important' look.

*

After school, on the way home through the park, they talked about the **DREAD SHED SCHOOL** and wondered who all these people were who were setting it up with Uncle Gobb. Malcolm remembered how Uncle Gobb had started to reel off his list and then stopped very suddenly in the middle of a word that began with a 'gee' sound.

'What was the word?' said Lizard.

'I don't know,' said Malcolm.

So there wasn't much more to say about that for the time being either.

Then they talked about the pond and the **PLOT OF LAND**, and Lizard got excited about catching stuff in the pond, but then she remembered that if she did catch stuff, she wouldn't have anywhere to put it.

'Are you and Dad staying in England for a long time?' said Malcolm.

'For as long as it takes,' Lizard said, in a voice that sounded very like Dad's, Malcolm thought.

He went back to thinking about Uncle Gobb nicking stuff from home, the **DREAD SHED SCHOOL** full of **facts** and **rich knowledge**, sitting in the middle of the car park, and Uncle Gobb marching about in and out of their school, taking children across to the toilets and … and … maybe playing in the pond on the **PLOT OF LAND** that Mr Keenly and Janet had discovered. Everything about the **PLOT OF LAND** that had sounded so good when Mr Keenly talked about it started to feel horrible. Uncle Gobb was going to be right in the middle of the pond place too, ruining everything.

'If,' he said, 'we could think of a way of getting rid of Uncle Gobb, that would stop him stealing things from home *and*, do you see, it would also close down the **DREAD SHED SCHOOL**. We have to stop it, don't we?'

'Or,' said Crackersnacker, 'we could concentrate on stopping the **DREAD SHED SCHOOL** happening, and Uncle Gobb would get so angry and fed up that he would … he would explode …'

'Or melt,' said Lizard.

'Or just keep quiet and leave me alone,' said Malcolm in a little voice.

Lizard said that she could help. Crackersnacker of course said he could help. Of course. Crackersnacker was the bestest most brilliantest friend anyone could have.

'That's good,' said Malcolm, rubbing his nose thoughtfully.

BOOM!

Smoke poured out of Malcolm's nose.

There was a flash, and a genie came through the smoke, out of his nose.

CHAPTER 10

Sha-Boom Flash, Sha-Boom Flash – GOOGLE!

'How did you like that?' said the Genie of Malcolm's Nose.

'What?' said Malcolm.

'That **BOOM**, that **FLASH**,' he said.

Crackersnacker snapped his fingers while he imitated the Genie of Malcolm's Nose saying, 'That **BOOM**, that flash; that **BOOM**, that **FLASH**; that **BOOM**, that **FLASH**.'

'No,' said the Genie, 'that's what I do and say, not what you do and say.'

'Who is this guy?' said Lizard.

'I, madam,' said the Genie, bowing low, 'am the Genie of Malcolm's Nose. I have come hither to be of assistance to Malcolm in his hour of need.'

Crackersnacker giggled. 'He's doing the old-book voice again, Malc.'

Malcolm was a little bit worried that he hadn't meant to summon up his Genie.

He had just been rubbing his nose thoughtfully.

'Your wish is my command,' said the Genie.

'Do we get a wish too?' said Lizard.

'No,' said the Genie. 'It's nothing personal. It's just that we genies stick with one person at a time. Malcolm is my person. Malcolm, again, I say to you, *your* wish is my command.'

Malcolm didn't know what to say. What wish did he have? He looked at Crackersnacker and Lizard for help.

Crackersnacker was still in the groove: 'That **BOOM**, that **FLASH**; that **BOOM**, that **FLASH** ...'

Lizard said, 'You could ask him to turn Uncle Gobb into a lizard.'

'No,' Crackersnacker said, 'we can't get him to do really big stuff to Uncle Gobb because Uncle Gobb has got his own genie, Doctor Roop the Doop, doop dee doop. And he's bigger and stronger than Malcolm's Genie ...'

'Yeah but remember, Crackersnacker,' said Malcolm, 'Doctor Roop the Doop went off in a huff while we were in America.'

'But was that a short huff, a long huff or a forever huff?' Crackersnacker asked. 'Big risk to take if it was a short huff and Doctor Roop comes back.'

'What about the **DREAD SHED SCHOOL**?' said Lizard. 'Can't you get him to stop that?'

'Sounds like big stuff to me,' said Malcolm. 'If I give him big stuff to do, he just says that he hasn't got enough Genie Juice or something. I tell you what, though: he's quite good on finding out things.'

'What?' said Lizard. 'Like Google?'

Crackersnacker liked that.

'Hah, "Like Google." SHA-BOOM FLASH, SHA-BOOM FLASH, GOOGLE; SHA-BOOM FLASH, SHA-BOOM FLASH, GOOGLE.'

When he said 'Google', Lizard said it with him.

'SHA-BOOM FLASH, SHA-BOOM FLASH, GOOGLE!'

'I've got about five seconds left,' said the Genie, 'before you miss this wish. If you miss a wish, I can't promise to turn up next time you rub your nose.'

'That's not fair,' said Crackersnacker.

'I don't make up the rules,' said the Genie. 'The rules are in 'The Great Book of Genie Rules'.'

'The genie rules!' said Crackersnacker. 'SHA-BOOM FLASH – the genie rules, yay.'

Malcolm started to go fizzy. This is what happened when things seemed to be whirring out of control all around him. It was all going wrong. Fizzy, fizzy, fizzy.

Lizard shouted out, 'Ask him what Uncle Gobb was going to say when he stopped in the middle of the word!'

The fizziness cleared and Malcolm shouted, 'What was Uncle Gobb going to say when he stopped in the middle of the word?'

The Genie stopped looking at himself in the mirror, looked up to the clouds, turned round twice and said, 'Genie.'

Malcolm, Crackersnacker and Lizard looked at each other.

They shrugged. Was that the answer to the question or was he just talking about himself again?

Lizard was on to it. 'Malc, listen, listen, man! Didn't you say that he was running through a list of people who were going to help him with the **DREAD SHED SCHOOL** when he stopped in the middle of the word? Did the word sound like the beginning of the word "genie"?'

Malcolm thought about it.

'Yes! He said, "gee".'

'Oh sheesh, Ponkyboy,' said Cracker-snacker, 'that means Doctor Roop the Doop is back and he's working on the **DREAD SHED SCHOOL**.'

Then as clearly as a clear bit of clear glass, Malcolm saw it. Fred Shed! Fred Shed was like a young, strong, thick-necked, glove-wearing Doctor Roop the Doop! Fred Shed *was* Doctor Roop the Doop, Uncle Gobb's genie!

That's why he had looked so familiar. And yet not familiar. He had disguised himself.

'Fred Shed is Doctor Roop,' Malcolm said to the other two. 'And this means

BIG TROUBLE!'

'I think my work here is over for today,' said the Genie. 'I appear once again to have been of great assistance. A little gratitude would go a long way, Malcolm,' he added.

Malcolm looked at him. What did he mean?

Lizard whispered, 'Thank him. He means, say "Thanks".'

'But he didn't say, "Say thanks",' Malcolm said anxiously.

Crackersnacker knew how to handle these Malcolm moments.

'Don't worry about it, Malc,' he said. 'Let's both say, "Thanks, man". I'll count us in, three, two –'

'Can I say, "Thanks, man" as well?' Lizard said.

'Sure,' said Crackersnacker. 'Here goes then. Three, two, one ...'

And all three of them said, 'Thanks, man.'

The Genie of Malcolm's Nose looked very pleased, smiled, checked his teeth in the hand mirror, muttered to himself, 'Yer lookin' good,

Apollo,' and disappeared
in a flash.

'We aren't any
nearer to getting rid of
the **DREAD SHED
SCHOOL**, are we?' said Malcolm, feeling sad
and desperate.

'Nope,' Lizard said.

'Nope,' said Crackersnacker.

Malcolm could see Uncle Gobb and this
Doctor Roop the Doop, doop dee doop, Fred
Shed genie doing whatever they wanted to do.
Things felt bad.

The problem was, things were about to
get a whole lot worse.

CHAPTER 11

A Whole Lot Worse
(Well, I did warn you.)

Mum said that as it was the last night that Dad and Lizard were sleeping in the **DREAD SHED**, before going off to the flat they had found round the corner, they could all have something to eat together. Crackersnacker came over too. And Dad's sister, Brenda the Mender, and her daughter, Wenda. And the dog was there.

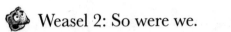 Weasel 2: So were we.

Weasel 1: We weren't.

Weasel 2: Look, we're here.

Weasel 1: I keep explaining. We're in the book. Not there. Not actually there.

Weasel 2: I don't get it.

At first, it sounded like it was getting better.

Brenda explained that things had got 'a bit tricky' at Wenda's school, and though it was a 'bit of a trek', Wenda would now be coming to Malcolm and Crackersnacker and Lizard's school.

Malcolm looked round the room to see

if anyone was going to ask what 'a bit tricky' at Wenda's school meant. No one did ask.

Uncle Gobb said, 'Things always get tricky for a reason, Brenda. There is always a reason.'

Wenda, who loved raisins, always carried raisins around with her and often shared her raisins with other people, then did her favourite raisin joke.

'Yes, Uncle Gobb,' she said, 'there's always a raisin.'

This really, really, really annoyed Uncle Gobb, who spelled out the two words, but he got them the wrong way round by mistake. 'Reason: r, a, i, s, i, n. Raisin: r, e, a, s, o, n. I hope that's clear, young lady.'

Wenda giggled. That made Cracker-snacker giggle. That made Malcolm giggle. That made Lizard giggle. Which made Uncle Gobb really, really, really angry.

'You see, Tessa,' he said, 'I try to put these foolish children right. Spelling is important. Spelling is a **fact**. It's an **important fact**. It's **rich knowledge**. But they don't see that. Just you wait and see. At my **DREAD SHED SCHOOL**, we will all know our spellings.'

'The only trouble is, Derek,' said Mum, 'you got it wrong.'

'Did I?' said Uncle Gobb. 'Oh no!'

He slumped forward in a state of deep despair that he had got his spellings wrong. He slumped forward straight into his plate of spaghetti. After a few seconds with his face deep in the spaghetti, he sat up again with one single strand of spaghetti stuck to his nose.

Mum leaned forward and carefully removed the bit of spaghetti.

Then Malcolm said the thing that made everything get a whole lot worse.

'In school today,' he said, 'Mr Keenly said that next to our school, there's this little "**PLOT OF LAND**"' – Malcolm did the wiggly underliney  thing here – 'and no one knows who it belongs to – perhaps to no one – and we might be able to get in there and find lizards and dragons and make tunnels and stuff.'

Crackersnacker kicked Malcolm under the table and nodded towards Uncle Gobb.

'Yeah, I know,' Malcolm said, thinking that Crackersnacker was talking about the nose-spaghetti.

So, Malcolm went on talking about the **PLOT OF LAND**. '… and isn't it amazing that it seems like it doesn't *belong* to anyone. It's just sitting there … We could climb trees and have paper dart competitions and explore and stuff …'

Dad liked the sound of that too.

'Hey, that's great, Malky,' he said. 'You could fix a tree trolley up there. You remember the one we had in Connecticut?'

Uncle Gobb was sitting up like a squirrel, his eyes shining, his nose twitching, concentrating very hard.

'Belongs to ... *no one*, you say, Malcolm?'

It was Crackersnacker's turn to be in despair. He knew it. He had seen it coming. The moment Malcolm started talking about the little **PLOT OF LAND**, he knew that Uncle Gobb would get interested in it.

He looked across at Lizard.

She nodded. She knew it too.

And now it was too late to get Malc to stop talking about it.

It was out.

And Uncle Gobb was on to it.

Surely, now, with Fred Shed – that is, Doctor Roop the Doop – and the 'people' – whoever they were – at , Uncle Gobb could get hold of the **PLOT OF LAND** for his **DREAD SHED SCHOOL**?

Crackersnacker needed to talk with Malcolm about this urgently. As soon as possible.

'Hey,' said Crackersnacker, looking across to Lizard and Wenda and then to Malc, 'why don't we go upstairs and look at that crazy video about people who turned into aubergines?'

That went down well with everybody.

Especially Uncle Gobb, who was now making plans.

Uncle Gobb breathed in and his cheeks filled with air. His great moment of triumph was about to happen. All he needed to do was talk to some people, who would talk to some other people, and something great would happen. It would be a **GREAT GOBB EDUCATION** thing.

Meanwhile upstairs, things were hotting up.

CHAPTER 12

Hotting Up

HEALTH WARNING

If this chapter gets too hot, take a step back, move away quickly and calmly. If necessary, place your hands under a cold tap and run the water for several minutes, then return to the book, and move swiftly on to Chapter 13.

END OF HEALTH WARNING

 Weasel 2: I'm feeling hot already.

 Weasel 1: That's because you're very furry.

 Weasel 2: So are you.

 Weasel 1: I know.

izard and Crackersnacker were trying to explain how they had seen the look on Uncle Gobb's face when Malcolm started to talk about the **PLOT OF LAND**. As Malcolm started to understand the terrible mistake he had made, things started to go fizzy again; his eyes started to go misty and his hands started to shake. He realised he had ruined everything. It was all his fault. *I blurted, didn't I?* he thought to himself. *That was me doing the blurt thing all over again.*

Wenda put her hand up to Crackersnacker and Lizard as if to say, 'stop going on about it'. 'Have a raisin, Malc,' she said.

Malcolm took a raisin and bit it very hard. Except it wasn't a raisin. It just *felt* like a raisin. In fact, it was the end of his tongue. He cried out in pain and his hands started shaking even harder, as if he was trying to shake them off the ends of his arms.

Everything was going wrong.

Crackersnacker, who was usually the brilliantest and unbelievablist at moments like these, wasn't really much help at all.

Instead, all he could see was what is called the 'Worst case scenario'.

Whatisa   Worst case scenario

Explanation from the book 'Great Worst Case Scenarios of the World'

A worst case scenario is what happens when you think of what could be the worst thing to happen.

Giovanni Scenario lived in Italy in 1520. He had three suitcases. One day, he was travelling across the beautiful town of Bologna with his three suitcases on his horse and cart. Suddenly, a rat ran out of a back alley. His horse rose up on his back legs, the cart tipped up and Giovanni Scenario and his three cases fell off.

Just then another horse and cart was coming along, and it rode over the three cases. Luckily, it missed Giovanni Scenario. People rushed over to help him up. People picked up his suitcases. One was a bit broken, one was a bit more broken, and one was very broken. His old friend Alberto Funghi handed it to him, saying

'This is the worst case, Giovanni Scenario.' Which later came to be known as the Worst Case Scenario.

End of Explanation of 'Worst Case Scenario'.

Crackersnacker told everyone about the **Worst case scenario** he was having. Uncle Gobb, he said, was going to take over their school.

All four of them could feel a panic coming over them.

Wenda stood up. She wanted to cool things down. So she said, 'Malcolm, we're going to need your Genie again.'

'Again? So soon?' Malcolm said sadly, still very, very, very, very sorry that he had made things worse. 'He might not be very strong.'

Lizard was tapping the top of her head. They looked at her, wondering if this would conjure up a great American genie. Or a great American lizard.

They waited.

It didn't.

She was just tapping the top of her head because she liked tapping the top of her head.

'I think,' she said, 'that Fender might come into this – you know, trees, a pond, a **PLOT OF LAND**, people talking to people to make things happen …'

Hmmmm … she does seem to know him very well, Malcolm thought. *He could be her … He could be her …*

He could hear Crackersnacker and Wenda saying something.

'Go on, Malc. Go on, stroke your nose …'

It was worth a try. So Malcolm stroked his

nose. There was a puff of smoke and out came the Genie.

'I am the Genie of Malcolm's Nose ...' he said.

'Does he have to say that every time?' Wenda asked.

'… and your wish is my command.'

'And that,' she said.

'Well, guys, what do we want?' said Lizard.

'Take the slow road, lady,' said the Genie, who seemed to talk in lots of different accents and voices, and was doing an American accent now. 'I don't deal with "guys". I deal with Malcolm and *only* Malcolm.'

Malcolm looked across to his three friends. They needed a really useful wish. Nothing too testing. And one that gave the Genie time to look in the mirror and admire himself.

Especially his muscles. And his hair. And his teeth.

'What we need,' said Wenda, 'is to get everyone in the school to know about what's happening.'

'Yeah, but even *we* don't know what's happening,' Malcolm said, still in despair.

'What we need, then,' said Wenda, chewing very carefully on a raisin, 'is we need to know what Uncle Gobb is really planning to do, so that then we can tell everyone, and then everyone will be really angry and do something about it.'

'Hey, that's really good,' said Cracker-snacker, who was pleased that someone was getting them all out of that huge panic they were in a few moments ago.

Yes, thought Malcolm, *that is really good.*

'I think Fender could do a —' Lizard was saying before the Genie pointed out something else: 'Since the last time I looked, I think my leg muscles have firmed up. Nice quads!' he said, admiring the quadriceps muscles on his legs.

'Last time you looked?' Crackersnacker said. 'That must have been about ten minutes ago.'

'Thou art a poltroon and a varlet,' the Genie said, turning away from Crackersnacker. 'I am counting down,' he warned.

Malcolm, who — thanks to Wenda, Lizard

and Crackersnacker – was feeling better, was quick on the button: 'OK, my wish is that you do that thing you do really well, which is go spying for us. We need you to find out exactly what it is that Uncle Gobb is planning …'

'Yeah,' said Crackersnacker. 'Is he going to take over our school?'

'You're not on this network, young man,' said the Genie. 'This is all about me and Malcolm, remember? Malcolm, I will do as you say: I will be a Holmes to your Watson.' And he disappeared in a flash.

'What was that about Holmes and Watson?' said Malcolm.

'Sherlock Holmes and Doctor Watson,' said Wenda. 'They live on Baker Street.'

'You know, lizards are much easier to figure out than you guys,' said Lizard.

CHAPTER 13

Gasp! Pant!
(A pant is not half a pair of pants.
It is something quite different. It's when
you breathe out making a noise. When you
say, 'A dog pants,' you don't mean a pair
of pants worn by a dog. You mean a dog
breathes out making a noise.)

Weasel 2: I think the dog would be glad to know about that.

Weasel 1: He's not here though. He's out with Mum.

Weasel 2: Will you tell him, then?

Weasel 1: I can't. He can't hear me.

Weasel 2: What a pity.

If you had been a traveller on the road between Malcolm's house and his school that evening, you might have seen a shed being pushed along the road by two men. One of them would have been small, with glasses and a red, shiny face, and the other one, big, strong, with a thick neck, with gloves on. The gloves were not on his neck.

They were on his hands. But you knew that.

And the traveller on the road might have wondered what was going on. But we're not travellers on that road. We are plumbers up to our knees in water.

OK, forget that last bit about the plumbers.

But we do know what's going on, don't we?

Uncle Gobb and Fred Shed (who is really Doctor Roop the Doop, Uncle Gobb's genie) are pushing the **DREAD SHED** to the school car park, to start the **DREAD SHED SCHOOL**.

'Why are we pushing this thing?' said Uncle Gobb, who surely, of all people, should know. 'Why can't you do your magic thing and just whizz it from here to there?'

'Because,' said Fred Roop, 'I need you to prove to me that you really believe in all that I do. You'll remember, I'm sure, what happened in America.'

'I'm sorry,' said Uncle Gobb. 'I've said I'm

sorry. I'm really good at saying sorry. I'm one of the best sorry-sayers around.'

'Yes,' said Fred Roop, 'but it's not enough for me for you to say sorry. I need to see you sweat for it. So, what we're doing is pushing the **DREAD SHED** all the way to the school car park. As you can see, I'm helping. I've given myself a very strong neck and some very fine gloves, while you are just a very small human being who would not be able to undertake this task on your own. Be grateful, little Derek Gobb, that I am of any assistance to you. Be patient. In time, when I have seen that you mean what you say and say what you mean, I will be of greater assistance to you.'

'Does that mean,' said Uncle Gobb, gasping and panting as the **DREAD SHED** got to a bit of a slope in the road, 'that you will help me –' **Gasp! Pant!** '– to seize the **PLOT OF LAND**, where you will help me build another **DREAD SHED** and another and another and another and *another and*

another ... so that Malcolm's school will be surrounded by my **GREAT GOBB DREAD SHED SCHOOLS**??!!! And they will in fact become not just schools but **THE GREAT GOBB DREAD SHED CENTRE COMPLEX INSTITUTE FOR IMPORTANT FACTS AND RICH KNOWLEDGE**, meaning we will, in the end, *take over* Malcolm's useless little school? –' **Gasp! Pant!** '– AND IT WILL BE ALL MINE!!!! **YESSSS!!!**'

Fred Roop was very powerful, but he didn't always catch on straight away when people talked to him quickly while gasping and panting. So he asked Uncle Gobb to say it all over again.

Which is just as well.

Just as well? How can it be just as well?

Surely we are now at a moment when Fred Roop more or less understands Uncle Gobb's evil plan and will make it happen for him? And Malcolm and Crackersnacker and Wenda and Lizard and Mr Keenly and Janet and all the people at the school will be crushed and defeated? How can that be 'just as well'? Eh? This is a bad, bad moment for our heroes, isn't it?

No.

How come?

Because – aha – the first time Uncle Gobb revealed his evil plan, he was telling it to Fred Roop and Fred Roop all alone. You might have hoped that Malcolm's Genie was somewhere nearby doing what Malcolm asked him to do, which was to spy. But Malcolm's Genie was nowhere near. He had stopped off at a shop that sells body-building food. But − and this is a very

good 'but' − by the time he got to Uncle Gobb, in order to spy on him, Uncle Gobb was telling Fred Roop the whole plan all over again!!!!!!!

So you see, just as well.

But surely Malcolm's Genie could be seen? And that would make Uncle Gobb say it all very quietly, so Malcolm's Genie wouldn't be able to hear it?

But no.

Malcolm's Genie was one step ahead. He had crept round the front of the **DREAD SHED** to where the door was – the very same door that Malcolm and Crackersnacker had once climbed out of – and crept inside the **DREAD SHED** so that he could hear everything without either Uncle Gobb or Fred Roop knowing!!! How brilliant and genie-like was that, eh?

And that was another reason why Uncle Gobb was gasping and panting so much. He and Fred Roop were not only pushing the **DREAD SHED** down the road. They were pushing the **DREAD SHED** *and* Malcolm's Genie … who, you will remember, had bulked up (which means that he was getting more and more muscly and extremely heavy).

This chapter finishes to the sound of

Uncle Gobb gasping and panting some more, without the slightest idea that he has just given away all the details of his evil plan. In fact, it is such an evil plan, it has become a **_PLOT._**

Gasp! Pant! Gasp! Pant!

CHAPTER 14

This Is Not a Chapter

This chapter won't actually tell you anything. It isn't really a chapter. What happens in this chapter (which isn't really a chapter), you see, is just what you would expect to happen. Malcolm's Genie brought the news of Uncle Gobb's plot to Malcolm, who, as you might expect, was with Crackersnacker, Wenda and Lizard. Then Malcolm, Crackersnacker, Wenda and Lizard told the plan first to Mum and Brenda and then to Dad.

So, in this chapter, you could, if you had wanted to, have nipped to the fridge and grabbed a snack. You wouldn't have missed anything.

CHAPTER 15

Wiry Little Creature with Long Fingers

Mum and Brenda were trying to make their printer work.

Printers are machines, but every now and then they get taken over by small, wiry creatures with long fingers. They sit inside the printer and make the printer print out things that no one has asked the printer to print, like a strange pattern with criss-cross lines. Or they make the printer die. The small wiry creatures kill the printer.

Mum and Brenda were in a fight to the death with one of these small, wiry creatures. Suddenly Brenda reached in, grabbed hold of one of the fingers of one of the wiry creatures, pulled the creature out and then flung it out of the window. The printer came back from the Land of Dead Printers, and started printing out just what Mum and Brenda has asked it to do. Which was a special notice saying: **UNCLE GOBB'S EVIL PLOT**.

TCHOOKA   TCHOOKA   TCHOOKA TCHOOKA, went the printer happily, while outside the window, the wiry creature with long fingers made whimpering noises. The dog watched it, just in case it tried to get back in. He would be on to it, all right.

CHAPTER 16

Mud

Dad was nodding. For a moment, it looked like he was nodding off to sleep, but he was just doing big American-guy nodding. Then he stopped doing big nodding, lifted up his hand into a high-five position and said, 'Put it there, guys,' and one by one, they gave him a high five.

Malcolm felt good that he could be proud of Dad. Other children in his class were sometimes proud of their dads, and now he could be proud of his dad too. Dad was going to do something to stop Uncle Gobb's **EVIL PLOT** happening. Dad was going to talk to Mr Keenly, Janet and Mrs Office. And Dad was going to talk to 'his people', who, he said were 'people-people' and usually backed anything that was good for 'people-people'.

Malcolm had no idea who Dad's 'people' were. He had no idea what 'people-people' were either, but he liked saying it: 'people-people', 'people-people'. Dad and the people-people. *Nice.*

Dad talked about tree trolleys and lizard dens and said he was pretty sure that the mud in the **PLOT OF LAND** was the kind of mud you could use to make things with and then put it in an oven and it would last forever.

'He means clay,' said Lizard helpfully.

Malcolm looked at Lizard. *The good thing about Lizard is that she can explain things. Yes, she may keep going on about lizards, but she does talk about other stuff too, and that's good.*

And saying 'That's good' to himself felt good too.

CHAPTER 17

Earwax

(The whole of Chapter 17 is not about earwax. You wouldn't find a whole chapter on earwax in any book, apart from maybe in a book for doctors about ears. One of the chapters in the book for doctors might be called 'Hearing', another might be 'Hairy Ears' and one might be 'Earwax'.)

I can see earwax in your ear.

No thanks.

You can have it if you like,

When Malcolm got to school the next day, the first thing he saw was the **DREAD SHED** in the car park. There was a sign outside that said:

THE GREAT GOBB DREAD SHED
SCHOOL FOR IMPORTANT FACTS
AND RICH KNOWLEDGE

Malcolm met Crackersnacker just by Uncle Gobb's school and they went up to the side of it and listened.

Uncle Gobb was teaching, and the children were asking him questions about **important facts**.

'Is earwax an **important fact?**' said one.

'No,' said Uncle Gobb.

'Is soup an **important fact?**' said another child.

'No,' said Uncle Gobb.

'Is the leak in the pipe going into our shower at home an **important fact?**'

'No,' said Uncle Gobb.

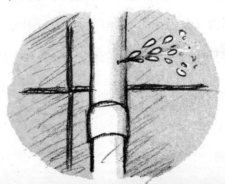

Crackersnacker looked at Malcolm.

'Not going very well at Uncle Gobb's **DREAD SHED SCHOOL FOR IMPORTANT FACTS** this morning,' said Crackersnacker.

'Do you think earwax is an **important fact?**' said Malcolm.

'It is important, if the earwax you're thinking about is important,' said Crackersnacker.

That's a very good point, Malcolm thought.

He hoped that Mr Keenly would ask them today to do some writing, and he would try to think of times and places when earwax was important and he would write about them.

Maybe Guy Fawkes's earwax was important. Guy Fawkes had so much earwax, he couldn't hear fireworks. Maybe.

In class, at the end of the day, Mr Keenly said he had an important announcement to make. Everyone went quiet. Mr Keenly said that he was worried. The half-term holidays were coming and he had found out that someone called Fred Shed had gone to see some important people and asked to be allowed to build something on the **PLOT OF LAND**. Janet said that this made her very angry.

Mr Keenly said, 'Thank you, Janet,' and they smiled at each other.

Then Mr Keenly said that the important people needed to decide if the **PLOT OF LAND** should go to the school or to Fred Shed. All they could do now was just wait and see.

'Nope,' said Lizard.

Mr Keenly was a bit surprised by that. He was even a bit annoyed by it. Lizard was a new girl, and he didn't like it when any child, especially a new one, just answered him back like that.

He was just about to say something quite stern and strict, when the bell rang. All the children streamed out of the school and there was a bigger than usual crowd of parents.

What's going on? thought Mr Keenly.

Crackersnacker whispered in Malcolm's ear, 'This is something really big, Ponkyboy. Massive.'

'Huge,' said Malcolm, who was excited and worried at the same time in a fluttery-inside sort of a way. He looked to see what was happening.

Mum and Brenda were in the middle of the crowd of parents, giving people the notice that the printer had eventually been allowed to print:

UNCLE GOBB'S EVIL PLOT.

Oliver's mum took one of the notices and stuck it under the door of the **DREAD SHED SCHOOL**.

A moment later, Uncle Gobb came out of the **DREAD SHED**, holding it in his hand.

'This is … this is … this is …'

It looked to Malcolm like he was boiling.

Uncle Gobb caught sight of Malcolm in the crowd and started shouting at him, '**THIS IS <u>YOUR</u> FAULT, ISN'T IT?** You did this. I don't know how you did this. I don't know how, but I know it's your fault. **I'VE BEEN TO CHINA**, and you wouldn't be doing this in China, I can tell you.'

'But isn't this your **PLOT** though?' asked Crackersnacker.

'That's not the point,' said Uncle Gobb.

'What *is* the point?' asked Wenda.

'Hey, that's a good question,' said Lizard.

'It's a terrible question,' said Uncle Gobb, beginning to wind himself up into one of his tornado rages.

Now, usually, when Uncle Gobb had one of his rages, Mum would say something like, 'That's all very well, Derek, but we're short of milk. Can you pop round to the shop and buy some?' But today, she didn't. That's because she was nearly as angry as Uncle Gobb. She didn't like his **EVIL PLOT**. She didn't like it that

Doctor Roop the Doop had got mixed up in it. And she didn't like it that the people – whoever they were – at  THE COW CLUB were mixed up in it too. And she really didn't like it that all this was invading Malcolm's school. Malcolm was doing very well at this school. Yes, he often found things difficult, but she was very pleased with how he was doing.

So, this time, just this once, Mum didn't say, 'Derek, we're short of milk, can you pop round to the shop and buy some?'

Instead, in the middle of Uncle Gobb's tornado, she said nothing. And Malcolm started to hear Freddy's mum, and Ulla's and Spaghetti's and Singalong's and loads of others, telling Uncle Gobb that they didn't want his **DREAD SHED** parked up in the car park and they didn't want his **DREAD SHED** in the *PLOT OF LAND*. And they didn't want THE GREAT GOBB DREAD SHED CENTRE COMPLEX INSTITUTE FOR IMPORTANT FACTS AND RICH KNOWLEDGE. And they didn't want him to be telling everyone what were or were not **important facts**.

In the middle of all that, Uncle Gobb shouted, 'I'VE BEEN TO CHINA. I know what I'm talking about!'

But then, Mr Yang said, 'I'm *from* China and it's not like that.'

And that brought Uncle Gobb to a standstill. He came to a complete and utter standstill.

Wow, thought Malcolm. *Uncle Gobb has come to a standstill, all because my Genie found out what Uncle Gobb's* **EVIL PLOT** *was and we told people and people told more people ...*

'It's not over yet, Ponkyboy,' said Cracker-snacker. 'He could still get his own way.'

'Really?' said Malcolm.

'He's only in one of his standstills for now. He could still get his people to wangle it and make his **EVIL PLOT** happen. He's got his genie AND THE COW CLUB people on his side.'

Oh no. Why does this sort of thing keep happening? thought Malcolm. *Good things, then bad things, then good things, then bad things.*

One moment Malcolm was feeling that it was all going well, and the next it was all feeling bad again.

Lizard and Wenda were standing there.

'What do you think?' he said to them.

Lizard tapped the top of her head.

Wenda took a raisin out of her pocket, put it into her mouth and started to chew it. Slowly.

Malcolm  got the point. A bad thing was coming along. Or was something even worse coming along?

CHAPTER 18

Now What? Or Not Now What?

It was all a bit tense around Malcolm's house around this time. Uncle Gobb didn't say much to Mum. Mum didn't say much to Uncle Gobb. Malcolm said nothing to Uncle Gobb and Uncle Gobb said nothing to Malcolm. Like I said, it was tense.

Weasel 2: It's very tense.

 Weasel 1: It's so tense you could balance a baked bean on it.

 Weasel 2: On what?

 Weasel 1: On the tense thing.

 Weasel 2: Oh … right. Yeah.

But Uncle Gobb was pressing on with his **EVIL PLOT**, even though no one wanted him to. That's why when he stood in front of the mirror, he said to himself, 'I'm looking quietly confident.' This is what football managers say when they think they are managing a good team: 'I am quietly confident.'

In fact, in the book 'Great Football Managers'

Sayings of the World', you'll find 'I'm quietly confident' along with 'Football's a game of two halves', 'A game's not over till it's over' and 'A team is only as good as the team'.

What Uncle Gobb didn't know was that Malcolm, Crackersnacker, Lizard and Wenda were plotting too …

CHAPTER 19

Only If It's Empty

'The thing is,' said Lizard, 'is … is … Uncle Gobb can only put his school on the **PLOT OF LAND** if it's empty.'

Lizard, Wenda, Crackersnacker and Malcolm were in Malcolm's bedroom.

'It's not empty,' Malcolm said. 'It's full of frogs and spiders and grass with arrows on the top.'

'Yup, I know. I meant empty of things that Uncle Gobb would think were in the way.'

'What? Like … people?' said Cracker-snacker.

'Well, it *is* empty then,' Wenda said. 'There aren't any people there. If Uncle Gobb is given the OK to put his **DREAD SHED SCHOOL** on the *PLOT OF LAND*, then **BOOM BOOM**, he wheels it up and puts it there. End of story.'

'Unless …' said Wenda, 'there *are* people there.'

'Do you mean imaginary people?' said Malcolm. 'Like in *Toy Story*?'

'Nope,' said Lizard, 'real people.'

'Right,' said Malcolm. 'So what we do is find some real people to be on the **PLOT OF LAND**.'

Crackersnacker jumped up and started flicking his fingers.

'Oh yes, I get this!' he said. 'I get this! You mean us, don't you, Lizard? I get this. We go and stand on the **PLOT OF LAND**. Isn't it us you mean?'

'That's no good,' said Wenda, 'because when we go off to get something to eat, or go home, Uncle Gobb will nip in there with his

DREAD SHED, and we've lost.'

'Not if we don't go off to get something to eat. Not if we don't go home,' said Lizard.

'Yes,' said Malcolm, 'we just stay there forever, like frogs.'

'Or lizards,' said Lizard.

Crackersnacker was still up and still flicking his fingers.

'Oh yes, I get this!' he said again. 'I get this ... Don't you see, Ponkyboy? A camp! You know, like Dad's, Fender's ... You know ... tents and stuff!!!'

There was the tiniest of tiny pauses while all four looked at each other and got what it was that Crackersnacker was talking about ... or was it what Lizard had been talking about? Or was it, in a way, what Malcolm was saying about living like frogs? Or was it, in a way, what Wenda was saying when she was saying that unless they were there all the time, Uncle Gobb would get in there quick with his **DREAD SHED**?

Whatever it was, it was a camp.

A camp!!!

But it was only a camp in their minds.

It wasn't a real camp.

Not yet.

They all looked at Malcolm.

'What?' said Malcolm.

'Nose, Malc,' said Crackersnacker. 'We can't do this on our own, and we can't ask any of the grown-ups to help us, because they'll say no.'

'What? Even Dad? Wouldn't he be able to help us?' said Malcolm, looking at Lizard, still wondering if he was her dad too. 'Hasn't he got tents and stuff hanging about?'

'Sure,' said Lizard, 'but they're about three thousand miles away in Connecticut.'

'That's a very long way,' Malcolm said.

'Important fact,'

said Crackersnacker, pretending to be Uncle Gobb.

'So,' said Wenda, 'it's the nose, Malcolm.'

So Malcolm got on with rubbing his nose.

Then came the smoke puffing out of his nose, followed straight after by the Genie.

'I am the Genie of Malcolm's Nose,' he said. 'Your wish is my command.'

'OK,' said Malcolm, 'we need some tents and some –'

But the Genie's mind was on other things.

'Look, guys,' he said, 'I've been doing some hard thinking. There's no point in my doing all this working out and body-building just for the sake of it. I need to do something with it: a sport. What do you think?'

'I don't know about that,' said Malcolm. 'We've got a whole heap of stuff that we need you to do.'

'Why's it always about you?' said the Genie. 'Don't I get a look-in? Haven't I got things that worry me, which I would like to sort out?'

'Yes, yes, I'm sure you have,' said Malcolm, looking at the others with a worried

look. 'But you do say, "Your wish is my command".'

'Oh yeah,' said the Genie, 'but that's just something I say. It comes from an old book: 'Great Genie Sayings of the World'. We all have to say that sort of thing or we get into trouble.'

'When you're in trouble, do you have to go and see Mrs Office, and stand outside her door?'

'Malc,' said Crackersnacker, 'the camp … the tents … remember? … Get him back to that …'

The Genie carried on thinking about getting into trouble.

'No,' he said, 'we are put in a room all

on our own where we have to think about what we've done wrong.'

'Oh yeah,' said Malcolm, 'I know. I hate that. I can never think what it is I've done wrong. And then … then …' he said, getting quite cross, 'they ask you to say sorry …'

'… and you don't know what you're supposed to be sorry for!' shouted the Genie, half laughing, half quite cross too.

Lizard whispered loudly, 'The tents, Malcolm. The tents.'

Wenda gave him a nudge.

'So, then,' said Malcolm, breathing in, 'I know it's not all easy for you today an' all that, but is there any chance you could help us do a camping thing on the **PLOT OF LAND** at my school?'

'Tents, you say?' said the Genie. 'Hmmm … how many?'

Lizard held up her hands. Did she mean ten?

She meant ten.

'Ten,' said Malcolm.

There was a long pause. The Genie seemed caught up in a dream for a moment. The children were feeling twitchy. It had seemed like an incredible plan. Risky, tricky, amazing … But now was it turning into a non-plan? A thing that flies by and flies off? Like a fly?

'Do you know where genies come from?' said the Genie.

'Er … no … yes … I mean no,' said Malcolm.

'Well, we usually turn up in stories that come from what these days is called the Middle East – but let's face it, everywhere's east of somewhere else in the end. And if everywhere's east, then you can't have a middle.'

'He's right, there,' said Wenda.

'Is he?' said Malcolm.

'What I'm saying,' said the Genie, 'is these tents you're after, they might look like the kinds of tents that come from where Genies once came from, hundreds of years ago.

ye genie tents of old.

I just need you to OK that, before I put in the order.'

Malcolm looked at the others.

Wenda gave the thumbs up.

Lizard gave the thumbs up.

Crackersnacker said, 'This is so amazing, Ponkyboy,' and whizzed round and round on one foot, while slapping his leg.

'OK,' said Malcolm.

CHAPTER 20

Tents. Or Is It Tense?

. . . That's why, one Saturday morning, when Uncle Gobb opened the front door of the **DREAD SHED SCHOOL FOR IMPORTANT FACTS AND RICH KNOWLEDGE** – where the pupils that Uncle Gobb had recruited for his school were doing their compulsory Saturday school **Important Facts** and **Rich Knowledge** session – Uncle Gobb saw something in the distance that stunned and amazed him.

Where before there had just been a fence and some trees, he could now see something very different: some tents. Not any old tents. The kinds of tents used by people who travel across the plains of Egypt, Iraq and Syria.

Uncle Gobb rushed back into the **DREAD SHED**.

'Do we have a telescope?' he shouted.

'No,' said the helper. 'A telescope is not an **important fact** for this age of child, Mr Gobb.'

'Binoculars?'

'Same, Mr Gobb,' said the helper.

'Then I will have to go down, myself, and find out what is going on.'

So, Uncle Gobb marched out of the car park, across the field, and up to the fence of the **PLOT OF LAND.**

He had been spotted coming. Lizard had a

telescope and called out,

So, by the time Uncle Gobb reached the fence, the children, who had been in and around their tents, were now standing on the other side of the fence.

The children were of course Malcolm, Crackersnacker, Lizard and Wenda, but also a few others had come to join them. Some you know already: Ulla and Spaghetti, Singalong, Freddy, Oliver … and others.

Uncle Gobb stood at the fence and said, 'It's no use. You lot are finished. You are the dregs. You are the nobodies. You are only interested in things that aren't important. You don't count. If you just stopped to think about it for a moment, I'M ON YOUR SIDE!'

'Well actually,' said Crackersnacker, 'you're on that side, and we're on this side.'

'That's a very good point,' said Malcolm.

Uncle Gobb shouted, 'Bah! A camp. What do you think that's going to do? Do you think it's going to stop me from creating the THE GREAT GOBB DREAD SHED CENTRE COMPLEX INSTITUTE FOR FACTS AND RICH IMPORTANT KNOWLEDGE?'

'Yes,' said Lizard.

'Oh it's you, is it?' said Uncle Gobb. 'I suppose this is your idea, is it? Yes, I remember the first time I saw you, covered in mud, in a camp in America. You and your blithering little CAMPS!!!' shouted Uncle Gobb, and he marched back across the field to the **DREAD SHED SCHOOL** in the car park.

'Now what?' said Malcolm.

'There doesn't always have to be a "Now what?"' said Lizard.

That night they made a fire and sang songs.

Malcolm's favourite was:

> 'I know an old bloke
> his name is Lord Jim
> he's got a wife who throws tomatoes
> at him
> Now tomatoes are juicy
> they don't injure the skin
> but these ones did,
> they was inside a tin.'

Malcolm loved that one.

He dozed off thinking of a tin of tomatoes flying through the air.

OUCH!

That would be as bad as a tin of baked beans flying through the air.

'Are you all right, Malc?' said Cracker-snacker, lying next to him in the tent.

'Yep.'

'It's just that you said, "Ouch!"'

'Ah yeah, it was the tin of tomatoes.'

'Right, you want to look out for them.'

'Right.'

THE APPENDIX TO CHAPTER 20

(So this isn't really a chapter.)

An appendix can be something you find in your belly – oh, hang on, don't look now. I mean, it's inside, and I don't want you to open up your belly to look. But believe me, it's there. Rather weirdly, it's there but doesn't have to be. It can be taken out. And nothing happens. So what's it there for? Nothing. Just hanging about being no use to anyone.

An appendix can also be a bit you tag on to a chapter or a book, where you say some extra stuff. In fact, it could be called An Extra. But it can't be called An Extra Appendix. No one wants an extra appendix.

OK, no one wants an extra appendix

apart from an appendix, who, I guess sometimes gets lonely and wants another appendix to talk to.

This appendix is for all the questions we have about the camp … like:

Where will the children get their food?

Will they get into trouble with their parents?

What will Mr Keenly say about it?

Will Mrs Office get angry with them?

Will the police come and arrest them and put them in prison?

… Any more?

Well, I can't hear you, but if you have got any more questions, please write to:

The Story Company

The Department of Questions

Storyville 43211

Imaginerica

ANSWERS:

The food came first from Mum, Brenda the Mender and Dad, but you see, all the other parents knew about Uncle Gobb's **EVIL PLOT**, didn't they? And they liked what the children were doing, so they also brought food for them. And sleeping bags. And teddies. And

then they took
the teddies back,
because the teddies
were embarrassing.

And if you're
wondering about where
they went to the toilet …
Brenda fixed up a portaloo.

As it was the half-
term holiday, Mr Keenly,
Janet, Mrs Office and
the other teachers weren't
worried about the children

bunking off school. Mr Keenly and Janet came to the camp one day with a cake. That was nice.

As for the police – well, that's an interesting one. We don't want to get too complicated here, but you'll remember that Mr Keenly said that the **PLOT OF LAND** doesn't BELONG (wiggly finger underliney thing) to anyone! So, there isn't anyone who can complain that some children have come along and put up a camp on THEIR land.

There's a blank page next, so you can write your other questions there.

CHAPTER 21

Hopeless

The camp on the **PLOT OF LAND** started to become famous. Well, so did Uncle Gobb's **DREAD SHED SCHOOL FOR IMPORTANT FACTS**. They were both famous.

People came from newspapers and TV to interview Uncle Gobb and anyone and everyone from the camp.

'Isn't this all rather hopeless?' said one interviewer, sticking her microphone through the fence.

Malcolm said, 'I'm not hopeless.' He turned to Crackersnacker. 'Are you hopeless?'

'No. I'm not hopeless.'

'I didn't ask that,' said the interviewer, getting cross. 'I said, "Isn't *this* all rather hopeless?"'

Singalong's nan, who had come to the camp for the day because she liked camps, joined in and said, 'We're not homeless. We've got our homes down the road and for the time being, this is our home too.'

'LOOK,' shouted the interviewer, 'I didn't ask you if you were homeless!'

'Then why say we are when we're not?' said Singalong's nan.

Uncle Gobb put on a very good show on TV, explaining that it was all about **important facts** and

rich knowledge. It all went really well until he was asked if blood was an **important fact**.

'Of course it is,' Uncle Gobb said, feeling a bit cross that he was being asked.

'So, can you tell me how the blood gets round the body?' said the interviewer.

'It goes,' said Uncle Gobb. 'It goes around.'

'How?' asked the interviewer.

'It goes from one part to another,' said Uncle Gobb.

'That's absolutely right,' said the interviewer, 'so I'm going to start in one part and you take the blood to another ... So here

I am, I'm a bit of blood and I'm in, say, the bottom-left part of the heart ... Where do I go next?'

'Look here,' said Uncle Gobb, 'blood isn't my subject.'

'But you said it was an **important fact**,' said the interviewer. 'If it's that important, why don't you know it?'

Uncle Gobb got up, said, 'I'VE BEEN TO CHINA,' and walked out.

Back at the camp, people were clustered round the portable TV that Brenda had set up, watching Uncle Gobb on TV. As Uncle Gobb said, 'I'VE BEEN TO CHINA,' Malcolm shouted, 'And so has Mr Yang!' and everyone cheered.

It was all getting very uplifting. This doesn't mean that anyone was getting lifted up. It means that everyone was feeling hopeful and excited.

Weasel 2: Why are they all in a camp?

 Weasel 1: So Uncle Gobb can't get into the **PLOT OF LAND**.

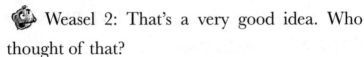 Weasel 2: That's a very good idea. Who thought of that?

 Weasel 1: I don't know.

 Weasel 2: Was it Dad's idea?

 Weasel 1: Have you been listening to this story?

 Weasel 2: I fell asleep.

Then came the Big Day.

'Massive, Ponkyboy,' said Crackersnacker to Malcolm.

CHAPTER 22

The Big Day
(A big day isn't any bigger than any other day. In its own way, that's an important fact.)

This Big Day was when it was going to be decided.

In the camp, Malcolm was confused. What did it mean 'was going to be decided'?

Wenda explained. 'This is *sooo* important, Malcolm. I mean, today is the day we're all going to find out who will get the **PLOT OF LAND**. Will it be Uncle Gobb's **DREAD SHED SCHOOL FOR IMPORTANT FACTS**? Or will we get it? You know, our school!'

'So who decides?' Malcolm asked.

'Some Wise People in a small room,' she said. 'Or, at least, these people say they are wise and everybody else believes they are,' she added.

Uncle Gobb had sent in his plan to the Wise People.

The school had sent in their plan to the Wise People.

The Wise People also knew about all the things that had been going on. They had seen the programmes on the TV.

It wasn't only the plans they were thinking about. They were thinking about what people had said on the TV. They were thinking about what it would look like to everyone 'out there' if they said yes to Uncle Gobb's plan rather than the school's … or what would it look like if they said yes to the school's plan rather than Uncle Gobb's … What would people 'out there' think?

Back at the camp, everyone clustered round the portable TV, waiting for the result to be announced.

'This is huge, Ponkyboy,' said Cracker-snacker.

'Well, whatever happens, whichever way it goes,' said Singalong's nan, 'I'm not going. I'm not leaving here.'

'No, neither am I,' said Spaghetti's dad.

'Nor me,' said someone else, and soon everyone was saying, 'Nor me,' 'Nor me,' 'Nor me.'

It was almost as if they thought that the Wise People in the little room could hear them through the TV.

Perhaps, in a way, they could.

So there everyone sat, waiting to find out which way it would go. People were so excited and worried about it, they went very quiet. They were breathing, but breathing quietly.

After ages and ages and ages of this, a TV person suddenly came running out of the building. Everyone looked up. She rushed to stand in front of the camera and said, 'I have it from a very reliable source …'

'What?' said Malcolm. 'What does that mean? What's Reliable Sauce?'

'Shhh,' said everyone.

'… that the decision goes to the school. The school will have the **PLOT OF LAND**.'

This was the biggest moment ever.

The camp erupted into a sea of shouting, cheering, towel-waving, kissing and hugging.

It had been decided: the **PLOT OF LAND** was going to belong to the school!!!!

Malcolm noticed that Lizard hugged him.

In the middle of the hug, Malcolm asked her, 'Is Fender your dad?'

'Yep,' said Lizard.

'We won!' shouted Crackersnacker. 'This is so massive, it's hugely massive, Ponkyboy.'

'Yeah!' shouted Lizard.

'Yeah!' shouted Wenda.

Malcolm was so amazed and delighted he didn't notice that he was rubbing his nose.

There was a puff of smoke and out came his Genie.

'I am the Genie of Malcolm's Nose,' he said. 'Your wish is my command.'

'Er, well, actually I haven't got a wish,' said Malcolm. 'I mean, it's all over.'

'Thanks to me,' said the Genie.

'Well, you were very helpful,' said Malcolm.

'And immensely bulky,' said the Genie.

'Yes, that too,' said Malcolm.

'What do you think of the tents?' said the Genie.

Malcolm was about to answer when just then, he saw somebody marching towards them. It was Fred Shed. Or rather it was Uncle Gobb's genie, Doctor Roop the Doop, disguised as Fred Shed. Stumbling along behind Fred Shed was Uncle Gobb.

'Uh-uh, trouble!' said Malcolm's Genie.

'Aren't you supposed to be a brave and muscly Genie?' Crackersnacker asked him.

'I am,' said Malcolm's Genie. 'Really I am, but not when I'm up against Doctor Roop the Doop. He's got loads more powers than me.'

By now, Fred Shed (that is, Doctor Roop the Doop) and Uncle Gobb had arrived at the camp on the **PLOT OF LAND**.

'So you win,' said Fred Roop.

'So you win,' said Uncle Gobb, peeping out from behind Fred Roop's back.

'I just said that myself,' said Fred Roop angrily to Uncle Gobb.

'I was just backing you up,' said Uncle Gobb.

'I don't need backing up!' shouted Fred Roop. 'I'm a genie. I am Doctor Roop! I am *the* Doctor Roop. The one and only Doctor Roop the Doop, doop de doop!'

'You don't need backing up,' said Uncle Gobb.

'I said that AS WELL!!!' yelled Fred Roop.

By now some more people had stopped dancing and singing and had come over to see what was going on.

'Are you trying to make a fool of me in front of all these people?' said Fred Roop, his eyes looking like they were breathing fire.

'No, no, really I wasn't,' said Uncle Gobb. 'Look, can we stop this? I think you're making a fool of me. '

It was now getting very, very awkward for everyone watching.

'Shall I tell you something, Gobb?' said Fred Roop, his voice sounding quiet but fierce. 'I was prepared to give you one more chance, but now you've blown it. So, this is what I'm going to say to you: there are no more chances left, for you, Gobb. You and me are history.'

'Wow!' whispered Malcolm's Genie to Malcolm. 'I have never seen a genie behave like that before.'

At that, Fred Roop turned and walked away and Uncle Gobb was left all on his own, with everyone staring at him.

No one knew what to say. Only a few minutes earlier, he had been everyone's arch enemy, but now he seemed like someone rather small, rather feeble and rather useless.

People started to feel just a bit sorry for Uncle Gobb. Of course, everyone was still angry with him for trying to take over the **PLOT OF LAND** for himself, but their anger was now mixed with this sorry feeling too. Even for Malcolm's mum, Tessa. And that's saying something. After all, she had put up with Uncle Gobb and all his plans with **DREAD SHEDS**, and Laetitia Bildungsroman's Tower in America. She had put up with him shouting at Malcolm at tea time, forever asking him questions and complaining about him. But even though she felt a bit sorry for him, Tessa wasn't saying to him, 'Come on, Derek, time to come home. I'll put on some tea, and you pop to the shop and get the milk.' So Uncle Gobb was just standing all on his own with all his plans in ruins ... but then – just then – there was a little movement among the people looking on.

It was Malcolm.

Malcolm could see that it was all over for Uncle Gobb and he stepped forward and walked towards his uncle.

Apart from a light breeze brushing the leaves in the trees in the **PLOT OF LAND**, everywhere was quiet.

When Malcolm reached Uncle Gobb, he stood in front of him, put his hand on Uncle Gobb's arm and said, 'Come on, Uncle Gobb, time to come home. I'll put on some tea, and you pop round to the shop and get the milk.'

Uncle Gobb, hardly seeming to realise it was Malcolm saying this and not Tessa, said, 'Yes, er ... yes. I will,' and off he went towards the shops, tapping his pocket to make sure he

had enough money in there for the milk.

Crackersnacker, Wenda and Lizard rushed over to Malcolm, and Crackersnacker put his arm round Malcolm and said, 'That was massive, Ponkyboy. Amazing. Huge.'

'Cool,' said Lizard. 'Really cool.'

And Wenda popped a raisin in her mouth and offered one to anybody who wanted one.

Everyone else drifted back to the tents to gather up stuff and clear up, chatting quietly among themselves about what they had just seen.

'I'm off to the gym,' said Malcolm's Genie. 'I need to pump some iron. I've got some serious work to do on my abs.'

'Yes,' said Malcolm to his Genie, 'and thanks for everything. You've been amazing.'

This stopped the Genie in his tracks.

'Have I? Really?' said the Genie, sounding a little unsure of himself.

'Yes, you have,' said Malcolm.

'Wow!' said the Genie. 'That's made my day,' and he smiled all over his face.

Off he went too, but not too fast, in case he bumped into Doctor Roop the Doop. That felt like something much too dangerous to face.

Malcolm's mum now joined Malcolm, Crackersnacker, Wenda and Lizard. She looked at them all very proudly and then said, 'What are we waiting for? Let's have this tea everyone's talking about.'

And off they all went.

On the way home, Malcolm had a thought and whispered to Crackersnacker about it.

'Do you think Uncle Gobb will stop doing all that bossy stuff now? You know, all the questions and telling us what to do?'

'I don't really know about that,' said Crackersnacker. 'We can hope he does, can't we?'

Malcolm was still worried.

'Do you think Uncle Gobb will ever come up with some new plan? Some new kind of **PLOT**? ' he said.

'No,' said Crackersnacker very definitely. 'Don't worry about it, Ponkyboy.'

APPENDIX

In this book there were some other books and points of interest. Here is some more information about them:

'Great Owl Pellets of the World'

A beautifully illustrated book showing in great detail all the stuff that owls sick up.

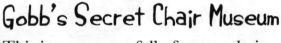

Gobb's Secret Chair Museum

This is a museum full of secret chairs.

'Great Things to Say When You Want to Sound as If The Thing You're Going to Do Next Is Really Easy'

Examples:

1. 'Might be sunny later.'

2. 'Might be rainy later.'

3. 'Might be sunny, might be rainy, later.'

'Great Lizards of the World'

Illustrations include:

1. Big lizard.

2. Bigger lizard.

3. Massive lizard.

'Great Floors of the World'

We are very sorry, but the greatest floors of the world are so great that there isn't room to show them here.

'Dictionary of the Very Worst Things to Say'

Examples:

1. 'There was a maggot in that apple you've just eaten.'

2. 'Weren't you nice once?'

3. 'There's a slug in your bed. Night, night!'

'The Great Book of Genie Rules'

Examples:

1. Clean your teeth.
2. When you say, 'Your wish is my command,' don't ever say, 'Your fish is my command.'
3. Jeanie Richardson from Edinburgh is not a genie.

'Great Worst Case Scenarios of the World'

One of the worst cases ever seen was on the railway train from Paddington to Bristol. It was made of yellow-and-purple-coloured cardboard and had stickers on it saying, 'I hate you'.

'Book About Earwax'

After forty years examining earwax in his laboratory in Norwich, Professor Henrik 'Steaming' Filibuster discovered that earwax tastes like Brussels sprouts.

'Great Football Managers' Sayings of the World'

Examples:

1. 'Football's a game, son.'
2. 'The game's not over till it's over, lad.'
3. 'If you want to score a goal, lad, the place to put the ball is in the net.'

'Great Genie Sayings of the World'

Examples:

1. 'If you want to go places, I've got a very nice flying carpet in the back of my van.'

2. 'Could be flu, could be a broken leg. How should I know? I'm not a doctor!'

3. 'I taught that Beyoncé how to sing.'

Malcolm, Crackersnacker,
Lizard and Wenda's

BIG BOOK OF
HOW TO STOP
UNCLE GOBB

Killer Questions to ask Uncle Gobb
when he starts shouting at us:

1. Where is the universe?

2. Where does the wind go?

3. What is nothing?

4. What is half a football?

5. Do sharks know that they are sharks?

6. What's the opposite of a tomato?

7. How far is it from one to two?

8. Where does your lap go when you stand up?

9. What does 'the' mean?

10. Why is it always today?

Bogus Killer Facts to stop Uncle Gobb telling us facts we don't want to know:

1. If a cat ate dog food it would turn into a dog.

2. If a dog ate cat food the cat would be hungry.

3. The Romans were called Romans because they were always roamin'.

4. The Saxons are called Saxons because they carried sacks.

5. The Normans are called Normans because all the men were called Norman.

6. The first genie was called Jeanie.

7. They've invented a new digital cure for sore eyes: an iPatch.

8. Cynthia Worshfall of Northwood, Middlesex, is so cold that she grows ice cubes in her armpits.

9. January 12, 1924, was abolished.

10. In the olden days they used to call a t-shirt a 'cup of tea shirt' because people used to put that kind of shirt on when they were having a cup of tea.

Obvious things to say to Uncle Gobb so that he'll run out the room shouting, 'I know, I know, I know! Tell them I know that, Tess!':

1. The Gingerbread Man is not really a man. He's made of gingerbread and men are not made of gingerbread. If men were made of gingerbread they wouldn't be able to speak because gingerbread can't talk.

2. A plate of spaghetti is not a plate made of spaghetti. The spaghetti is on the plate. If a plate was made of spaghetti it would be all floppy and soggy and you couldn't wash it up later because all the spaghetti would flop

around in the sink and in the end break up into little bits of spaghetti.

3. The North Pole is not a pole.

4. The South Pole is not a pole either.

5. If the South Pole was a pole, it would be really unfair for the North Pole to be NOT a pole while the South Pole was going about saying, 'I'm a pole.'

6. There is no such thing as bedtime. If you're a bed, it's always bedtime. Bedtime is the time you're a bed, which is all the time. If you throw away an old bed then it's not bedtime anymore.

7. When you say two times two, you get four. That's a big change. But one times one is one. Nothing's changed. So there really isn't much point in having one times one. It's like saying, 'Hey, do you know that the same is the same?' Or, 'Hey, you see this table? It's a table.' We know it's a table! You said it was a table so it's a table! One times one is one. OK, we know that.

8. Charles Dickens wrote a book called *A Christmas Carol* but it's not about someone called Carol. It's about someone called Scrooge. It might have been better if he had

called it *A Christmas Scrooge* then no one would make the mistake of thinking it was about someone called Carol.

9. 'Tough' rhymes with 'stuff'. 'Cough' rhymes with 'toff'. 'Bough' rhymes with 'cow'. 'Through' rhymes with 'too'. 'Though' rhymes with 'toe'. That means 'tough', 'cough', 'bough', 'through' and 'though' don't rhyme with each other. If you think 'cough' rhymes with 'bough' you might end up saying things like, 'I've got a really bad cow,' when you meant to say, 'I've got a really bad cough.' And that wouldn't be true, unless as well as

having a bad cough, you had a bad cow.

10. Not everything is a lizard. (Lizard wrote this one.)

PROFILES

Michael Rosen

Michael was born and brought up in a flat but this didn't make him flat. He is not flat. He now lives in a house that isn't a flat, and the house isn't flat either. In fact, so far nothing in this profile of Michael Rosen is flat. Now here comes a flat bit. When Michael sings, he often sings flat. That means singing a tiny bit too low. Like when you want to go for a walk under the sofa but it's too low. Michael has never walked under a sofa.

Neal Layton

Neal started drawing, painting and writing a long time ago. Not as long ago as the Romans. Or the Saxons. Or the Normans. The Romans, Saxons and Normans wore helmets. Neal does not wear a helmet, not even when he's drawing, painting and writing. You could say that Neal is an artist. You could also say that because he draws he's a drawer. The trouble with saying that, though, is that you might think he's someone who lives in a chest of drawers. Neal does have a chest but that doesn't mean that he's a chest of drawers.

Make sure you haven't missed:

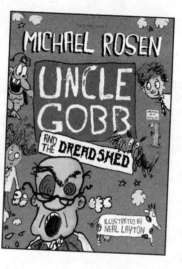

Young person! Yes, you! Put this book down **IMMEDIATELY** and do some homework! You must **NOT** read about my nephew Malcolm and the city of Ponky and Genies and weasels and my **DREAD SHED**.

There is nothing **SENSIBLE** in this book!

Child! If you read this book then I will test you afterwards. You must answer all these questions:

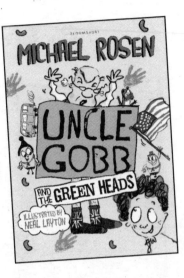

1. How do I plan to get rid of my nephew Malcolm once and for all?

2. Who is Brenda the Mender?

3. Why doesn't my Genie help me?

If you get them wrong, you must do **MORE HOMEWORK**.

Uncle Gobb, founder of